hould be returned to any bran
library on or befor

Note to parents, carers and teachers

Read it yourself is a series of modern stories, favourite characters and traditional tales written in a simple way for children who are learning to read. The books can be read independently or as part of a guided reading session.

Each book is carefully structured to include many high-frequency words vital for first reading. The sentences on each page are supported closely by pictures to help with understanding, and to offer lively details to talk about.

The books are graded into four levels that progressively introduce wider vocabulary and longer stories as a reader's ability and confidence grows.

Ideas for use

- Although your child will now be progressing towards silent, independent reading, let her know that your help and encouragement is always available.

- Developing readers can be concentrating so hard on the words that they sometimes don't fully grasp the meaning of what they're reading. Answering the puzzle questions on pages 46 and 47 will help with understanding.

For more information and advice on Read it yourself and book banding, visit **www.ladybird.com/readityourself**

Book
Band
10

Level 4 is ideal for children who are ready to read longer stories with a wider vocabulary and are eager to start reading independently.

Special features:

Clear type

Longer sentences

Detailed illustrations to capture the imagination

Full, exciting story

Richer, more varied vocabulary

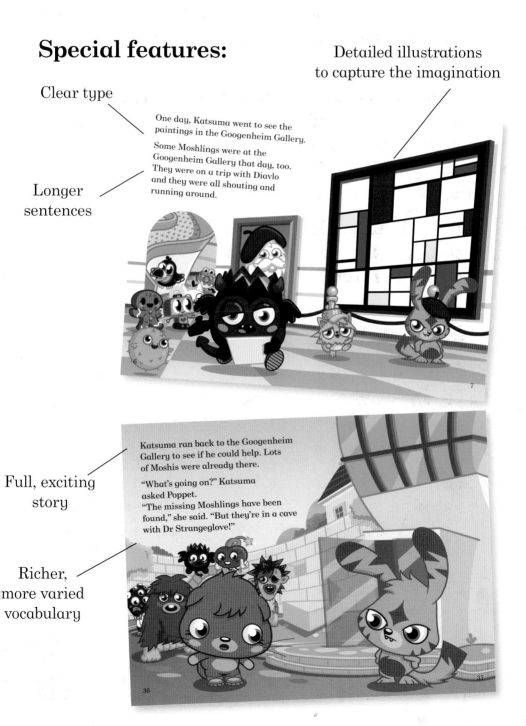

One day, Katsuma went to see the paintings in the Googenheim Gallery.

Some Moshlings were at the Googenheim Gallery that day, too. They were on a trip with Diavlo and they were all shouting and running around.

Katsuma ran back to the Googenheim Gallery to see if he could help. Lots of Moshis were already there.

"What's going on?" Katsuma asked Poppet.
"The missing Moshlings have been found," she said. "But they're in a cave with Dr Strangeglove!"

Educational Consultant: Geraldine Taylor
Book Banding Consultant: Kate Ruttle

A catalogue record for this book is available from the British Library

This edition published by Ladybird Books Ltd 2013
80 Strand, London, WC2R 0RL
A Penguin Company

001

The moral right of the author and illustrator has been asserted.

Ladybird, Read It Yourself and the Ladybird Logo are registered or
unregistered trademarks of Ladybird Books Limited.

ISBN: 978-0-72327-397-4

Printed in China

Katsuma
and the Art Thief

Written by Ronne Randall

Illustrated by Fran and David Brylewska

One day, Katsuma went to see the paintings in the Googenheim Gallery.

Some Moshlings were at the Googenheim Gallery that day, too. They were on a trip with Diavlo and they were all shouting and running around.

All at once, Gingersnap tripped! He landed with his paws right on one of the paintings.

"Gingersnap, get away from that painting!" shouted Diavlo, as the alarm went off.

When Gingersnap took his paws away, there was paint all over them and some of the painting was missing!

"That painting must still be wet!" thought Katsuma. "But how can it be, when it's been here for so long?"

The gallery director came to look at all the paintings. They were ALL still wet!

"These paintings aren't real," the director said. "A thief must have taken the real paintings and put fake paintings on the walls!"

Katsuma said, "If the fake paintings are still wet, the thief must have just put them here."

"How can we get the real paintings back?" the director asked.

"I'll find a way!" said Katsuma.

First, Katsuma went to wash off the paint. When he came back from washing, his hat was missing.
"A thief has taken my hat!" he said.

Katsuma thought he saw someone going towards the gallery entrance, and he went to look. Too bad he didn't see the banana skin on the floor! "Help!" shouted Katsuma.

Katsuma grabbed the sign at the gallery entrance. He could then see some footprints on the floor, going towards the Hall of Fame.

21

With one big jump, Katsuma landed right in the Hall of Fame. He followed the footprints to a room where he found two little tunnels.

He kept going down the long tunnel until he came to a reading room.

Katsuma opened the door and all at once a big splash of Toad Soda came right at him!

"First my hat, then the banana skin and now Toad Soda. Someone wants to get me!" he said.

In the reading room, Katsuma
found a big magnifying glass.
"Just what I want!" he said.

With the magnifying glass,
Katsuma looked at the paw prints
in the Googenheim Gallery.
"These aren't paw prints," he said.
"They are GLOVE prints!"

29

Now Katsuma knew just who he was looking for – Dr Strangeglove! And he knew who could help – Elder Furi. Katsuma went to find him.

"My Super Moshis are already looking at Dr Strangeglove's paint in a secret lab," Elder Furi told Katsuma.

33

Elder Furi took Katsuma to the secret lab.

"We've found that Dr Strangeglove's paint can hypnotize Moshlings," said Elder Furi. "Lots of Moshlings are already missing!"

Katsuma ran back to the Googenheim Gallery to see if he could help. Lots of Moshis were already there.

"What's going on?" Katsuma asked Poppet.
"The missing Moshlings have been found," she said. "But they're in a cave with Dr Strangeglove!"

37

Poppet told Katsuma that
Dr Strangeglove had hypnotized
all the Moshlings so he could
glump them.

Katsuma knew where the cave
was. "I have to stop him!" he said,
rushing off.

Katsuma's long day was over.

"It turned out all right," he thought. "It's just too bad that Dr Strangeglove is still out there. But one day someone will stop him – and I want that someone to be me!"

GOOGENHEIM
ART GALLERY

How much do you remember about the story of Moshi Monsters: Katsuma and the Art Thief? Answer these questions and find out!

- Where does Katsuma go to see some paintings?

- Which Moshling trips and lands on a painting?

- What is wrong with all the paintings?

- Who has stolen the paintings and replaced them with fake ones?

- Where does Elder Furi take Katsuma?

- What does Dr Strangeglove's special paint do to the Moshlings?

Unjumble these words to make characters from the story, then match them to the correct pictures.

Kusamat   Peptop   Erdel Friu

rD Saggorntelve   Gransipeng

Read it yourself with Ladybird

Tick the books you've read!

For more confident readers who can read simple stories with help.

Level 3

Longer stories for more independent, fluent readers.

Level 4